♥ for Mia Rae ♥

Seb ✗

First published in 2016 by Child's Play (International) Ltd
Ashworth Road, Bridgemead, Swindon SN5 7YD, UK

Published in USA by Child's Play Inc
250 Minot Avenue, Auburn, Maine 04210

Distributed in Australia by Child's Play Australia Pty Ltd
Unit 10/20 Narabang Way, Belrose, Sydney, NSW 2085

ISBN 978-1-84643-759-5
L141015CPL04167595

Printed in Heshan, China

1 3 5 7 9 10 8 6 4 2

A catalogue record of this book
is available from the British Library

www.childs-play.com

MAYDAY
Mouse

Seb BRAUN

One bright, sunny day,
Captain Mouse built a little
boat out of a walnut shell,
a toothpick and a handkerchief.

"It's my brother's birthday,"
she told her friends.
"I'll take his present by boat."

"Bon voyage!" they all shouted.
"Watch out for big waves and watery perils!
If you need help, just shout MAYDAY!"

The sun shone.

"What a lovely day for sailing."

"There won't be any big waves
or watery perils today!"

But then the breeze dropped. The little boat stopped.

"Never mind!" thought Captain Mouse.

"I'll just whistle up a wind."

And she whistled a sea shanty three times.

The wind picked up again.

"That's better!" smiled Captain Mouse.

The wind became stronger.

"Whee!" sang Captain Mouse.

"This is fun!"

The little boat bobbed up
and down, and raced along.

"I'll be there in no time," said Captain Mouse.

Then it started to rain
and the boat filled with water!
Captain Mouse held tight on to
the mast and her brother's present.

"What's happened to my sail?"

Thunder roared
and lightning flashed
across the sky.

"Oh no!"
thought Captain Mouse.

"Here come the big waves
and the watery perils!"

The little boat flew through the air.

"What's that crashing noise I can hear?"

thought Captain Mouse.

"It's getting closer! What can it be?"

"It's a dark and dangerous cave!" she squealed.

"I'd better stay clear of it!"

But no sooner was she past the cave
than Captain Mouse saw that she was
heading straight for some terrible rocks!

She hit them with a horrible crash!
Captain Mouse, her brother's present,
her little walnut shell boat, her toothpick
mast and her handkerchief sail were all
thrown high into the air!

"This is the end of me!" she thought.

Captain Mouse was soaked through. She was cold and tired.
She fell fast asleep.

The water rose, and the island became smaller and smaller.

Captain Mouse woke up and shook the water from her fur.

"That's better," she thought. "The rain has stopped.

The sea is calm again. What I need is a plan."

Captain Mouse tied her flag to the broken mast.

She shouted at the top of her voice.

"MAYDAY! MAYDAY! Help! Help!"

Finally, she heard a buzzing
and a splashing.

"We heard you shouting!"
called Dragonfly and Frog.
"Then we saw your flag."

"Look what we've brought
for you!" they cried.
"Half a cork to make a boat.
A coin for a keel.
A toothpick for a mast.
And a leaf for a sail!"

Captain Mouse set to work.

She pushed the mast
into the cork.

She fixed the leaf onto the mast.

"Hurrah!" she laughed.

"I'm ready to sail again!"

The breeze filled the sail and the little
cork bobbed over the waves.

"Farewell!" called Dragonfly and Frog.
"Be careful! We're here if you need us!"

The sun shone. The gentle breeze
blew the little boat along. And this time,
there were no big waves or watery perils.

Captain Mouse jumped ashore,
happy to see her brother at last.

"I've just had such a scary adventure!
There were big waves,
and watery perils like rain
and caves, and terrible rocks
and a shipwreck – and EVEN
a desert island!"

"Wow! All this way to bring me a present!
Can you sing me HAPPY BIRTHDAY too?"

So everyone did!